Yoga & Pilates

An Integrated Life of Fitness

Core Workouts

Cross-Training

Eating Right & Additional Supplements for Fitness

Endurance & Cardio Training

Exercise for Physical & Mental Health

Flexibility & Agility

Sports & Fitness

Step Aerobics & Aerobic Dance

Weightlifting & Strength Building

Yoga & Pilates

An Integrated Life of Fitness

Yoga & Pilates

SARA JAMES

Mason Crest

Mason Crest
450 Parkway Drive, Suite D
Broomall, PA 19008
www.masoncrest.com

Copyright © 2015 by Mason Crest, an imprint of National Highlights, Inc. All rights reserved. No part of this publication may be reproduced or transmitted in any form or by any means, electronic or mechanical, including photocopying, recording, taping, or any information storage and retrieval system, without permission from the publisher.

Printed and bound in the United States of America.

First printing
9 8 7 6 5 4 3 2 1

Series ISBN: 978-1-4222-3156-2
Hardcover ISBN: 978-1-4222-3166-1
Paperback ISBN: 978-1-4222-3204-0
ebook ISBN: 978-1-4222-8704-0

Cataloging-in-Publication Data on file with the Library of Congress.

3 4859 00354 5273

CONTENTS

Introduction	6
1. What Are Yoga and Pilates?	9
2. How Do Yoga and Pilates Contribute to Fitness?	27
3. Gear and Safety for Yoga and Pilates	37
4. What Other Benefits Do Yoga and Pilates Have?	51
Find Out More	59
Series Glossary of Key Terms	60
Index	62
About the Author and the Consultant & Picture Credits	64

KEY ICONS TO LOOK FOR:

Text-Dependent Questions: These questions send the reader back to the text for more careful attention to the evidence presented there.

Words to Understand: These words with their easy-to-understand definitions will increase the reader's understanding of the text, while building vocabulary skills.

Series Glossary of Key Terms: This back-of-the book glossary contains terminology used throughout this series. Words found here increase the reader's ability to read and comprehend higher-level books and articles in this field.

Research Projects: Readers are pointed toward areas of further inquiry connected to each chapter. Suggestions are provided for projects that encourage deeper research and analysis.

Sidebars: This boxed material within the main text allows readers to build knowledge, gain insights, explore possibilities, and broaden their perspectives by weaving together additional information to provide realistic and holistic perspectives.

INTRODUCTION

Choosing fitness as a priority in your life is one of the smartest decisions you can make! This series of books will give you the tools you need to understand how your decisions about eating, sleeping, and physical activity can affect your health now and in the future.

And speaking of the future: YOU are the future of our world. We who are older are depending on you to build something wonderful—and we, as lifelong advocates of good nutrition and physical activity, want the best for you throughout your whole life.

Our hope in these books is to support and guide you to instill healthy behaviors beginning today. You are in a unique position to adopt healthy habits that will guide you toward better health right now and avoid health-related problems as an adult.

You have the power of choice today. We recognize that it's a very busy world filled with overwhelming choices that sometimes get in the way of you making wise decisions when choosing food or in being active. But no previous training or skills are needed to put this material into practice right away.

We want you to have fun and build your confidence as you read these books. Your self-esteem will increase. LEARN, EXPLORE, and DISCOVER, using the books as your very own personal guide. A tremendous amount of research over the past thirty years has proven that the quality of your health and life will depend on the decisions you make today that affect your body, mind, and inner self.

You are an individual, liking different foods, doing different things, having different interests, and growing up in different families. But you are not alone as you face these vital decisions in your life. Those of us in the fitness professions are working hard to get healthier foods into your schools; to make sure you have an opportunity to be physically active on a regular basis; to ensure that walking and biking are encouraged in your communities; and to build communities where healthy, affordable foods can be purchased close to home. We're doing all we can to support you. We've got your back!

Moving step by step to healthier eating habits and increasing physical activity requires change. Change happens in small steps, so be patient with yourself. Change takes time. But get started *now*.

Lead an "action-packed" life! Your whole body will thank you by becoming stronger and healthier. You can look and do your best. You'll feel good. You'll have more energy. You'll reap the benefits of smart lifestyle choices for a healthier future so you can achieve what's important to you.

Choose to become the best you can be!

—Diana H. Hart, President
National Association for Health and Fitness

Words to Understand

 ***abdominal:*** Having to do with or located near the part of your body that contains your stomach and intestines.

Chapter One
What Are Yoga and Pilates?

Different people choose different ways to get fit. Some train for 5Ks and marathons. Other people join sports teams, having fun and getting fit along the way. Still other people join gyms; they lift weights to build strength and work out on the elliptical machines.

Yoga and Pilates are two more ways to get fit. Both are systems of movements that increase flexibility and strength. Anyone can practice yoga and Pilates for fitness, and both are great ways to exercise.

Although many people enjoy yoga simply as a relaxing form of exercise, yoga is actually an ancient spiritual practice. According to writings from more than two thousand years ago, yoga is "union of the self with the Divine."

Yoga & Pilates

WHAT'S THE DIFFERENCE?

Yoga and Pilates are similar, but there are some important differences. You may end up liking one more than the other, so check out both!

Yoga is the older tradition with ancient roots that stretch back many thousands of years. When you practice yoga, you complete a series of postures called *asanas*. Every posture has a name in Sanskrit, an ancient Indian language, as well as in English. The names often correspond to what the poses make your body look like, such as cobra, cat, or triangle poses. Different poses can be done standing up, sitting down, or lying down.

Breathing is very important in yoga. You'll focus on your inhalations and exhalations to make them deeper and steadier, which affects all sorts of things like heart rate and stress. You may be asked to "breathe into" your muscles during poses, which will help you relax into them.

There's more to yoga than just physical movements and breathing. Meditation and even spirituality can be important components of yoga too. Meditation is the practice of relaxing the mind and concentration on the present moment. People can practice meditation without practicing yoga, but you will get a taste of meditation from doing yoga. Most yoga practices end with something called *savasana*—a short meditative pose that involves lying down relaxed on the ground.

Pilates is a more modern invention, and was actually inspired partly by yoga. Pilates also involves going through a series of poses, although they do not have Sanskrit names. The poses in Pilates are more focused on the core muscles (the ones in the center of your body rather than the muscles in the arms and legs). Most Pilates poses are done while lying on the ground.

Breathing is significant in Pilates as in yoga, but physical movement ends up being the most important thing to concentrate on. Meditation also doesn't have a central place in Pilates, although a connection between the body and the mind is still important.

This Indian painting from the early 1600s shows seven men practicing yoga under a banyan tree.

Yoga & Pilates

AN ANCIENT TRADITION

Yoga has become really popular in North America in the last few years. However, yoga has a long history that reaches back many thousands of years. To understand the origins of yoga, you have to go back a long way—3,000 to 5,000 years, in fact! We don't exactly know when yoga was created, since people were practicing yoga even before they were writing. Yoga means "to join or yoke together," referring to the mind and the body. Early yoga practitioners wanted healthier, stronger minds back then, just like they do today.

The first evidence of yoga comes from some stone carvings of figures doing yoga found in the Indus Valley. The stone carvings are around 5,000 years old, though older evidence might still be found someday. Then, once writing came along, people started writing about yoga.

Yoga isn't rooted in any particular religion, and it's not a religion itself. Hinduism and Buddhism, along with other religions, adopted some yoga principles, but they came after the creation of yoga. Yoga doesn't involve worshipping a god or gods, but it has been used in religions for that purpose.

The Vedas—the sacred scriptures of Hinduism written somewhere between 1500 and 1000 BCE—talk about yoga. Later on, more scriptures called the Upanishads continued to describe yoga in relation to Hinduism. Even later (around 500 BCE), a text called the Bhagavad-Gita described yoga practice in detail and set out some of the main types of yoga practice at the time. A scholar named Patanjali also wrote a book called *Yoga Sutras* many hundreds of years ago, which built on the earlier Hindu works. He recorded popular thoughts about yoga and ways to practice yoga. Yoga students today still follow the same principles and practices today.

For a long time, yoga was only practiced in Asia. In the late 1800s, though, it traveled to the United States. It became really popular in the 1960s, as people became more interested in Asian religion and ways of life, and Indian yoga teachers traveled to the United States. More

When Europeans began venturing into the East, they discovered people doing yoga in India. This drawing was made by one of these travelers.

Yoga & Pilates

Make Connections: The Eightfold Path of Yoga

Patanjali came up with eight different parts of yoga, all of which were important to really make the most of yoga practice. They are *yama* (social restraints and ethical values), *niyama* (purity, tolerance, and study), *asanas* (physical movement), *pranayama* (control of breath), *pratyahara* (meditation preparation), *dharana* (concentration), *dhyana* (meditation), and *Samadhi* (realization of the self).

and more people picked up yoga every year, so that today, millions of people practice it. The Yoga in America Study 2012 conducted by the *Yoga Journal* estimated that 20.4 million people practice yoga!

STYLES OF YOGA

There are many different styles of yoga, from more calm and relaxed types to more active ones. Here are a few:

- *Hatha.* One of the most popular styles today in North America, and the style that most students start with, it involves slow, fluid movements along with breathing. Yogi Swatmarama in India created Hatha yoga in the 1400s.
- *Iyengar.* Similar to Hatha, but the poses are generally held for longer. More equipment is used, and practitioners pay more attention to balance and proper body alignment.
- *Ashtanga.* More of a workout than other types of yoga, and quicker than others too. Ashtanga yoga focuses more on the physical side of things, rather than meditation or mental calm.

What Are Yoga and Pilates?

Yoga has been called "meditation in motion," because the movements are designed to create a deeper awareness and consciousness.

16   Yoga & Pilates

Downward dog is one of yoga's simpler poses.

- *Bikram.* This type is also called hot yoga, since it is done in a room heated to about 105 degrees. The poses are similar to Hatha yoga, but they are more challenging because of the heat. Each Bikram class goes through the same set of postures.
- *Kundalini.* A faster and more repetitive type of yoga that goes through poses very quickly, though still aligned with breathing.

What Are Yoga and Pilates?

Modern Pilates classes often use giant balls like these to support some of the poses.

- *Yin.* Much slower than most other forms of yoga. Practitioners hold each pose for five minutes or more, to work on the health of connective tissues (tendons and ligaments) rather than muscles.

Yoga & Pilates

SOME YOGA POSES

Yoga has hundreds of poses to choose from. Some are more familiar to yoga students, and make up basic practices. They may be hard at first, but with practice, they get easier! There's downward dog, in which you place your feet and hands on the floor and make a triangle with your body, with your hips pushing back. Child's pose involves sitting on your heels while stretching your arms forward on the ground. Both of those asanas are considered resting poses, used in between other, more active poses, such as warrior 1, which requires you to bend one knee in front of you at a ninety-degree angle while keeping your other leg stretched straight out behind you with that foot flat on the floor. Your arms reach up toward the sky, while your chest and heart point out and up. Foot balances are common, too, where you balance on one foot while keeping the other one tucked in above the ground, as in tree pose.

Then there are the extremely difficult poses that require a lot of strength and concentration. Beginning yoga students will probably not be able to do arm balances that place all the body's weight on the arms. Or back bends, which require spine flexibility and arm strength. Flexibility and strength improves with time, though, so that students can work up to more challenging asanas as time goes on.

A NEWER INVENTION

Pilates is a much newer invention than yoga. A man named Joseph Pilates, who was born in Germany in 1883, invented this system of exercise. He was sick as a child, which inspired him later in life to work hard at building his fitness so that he could spend the rest of his life healthy and strong. He practiced martial arts, yoga, and bodybuilding, among other things.

During World War I, Pilates was living in England. Since he was German, and the English were fighting the Germans, he was imprisoned for a time. He spent that time coming up with a formal system of

The teaser pose is a great way to build strong stomach muscles.

Yoga & Pilates

exercise, which he taught to other people imprisoned with him. This was the forerunner of the Pilates system.

After the war, he returned to Germany and spread his new form of exercise by teaching it others. When he moved to New York City in 1926, he opened a fitness studio. At first, his system was most popular with dancers, both in Europe and in the United States. In fact, that's how Pilates first spread around the country, as dance instructors taught students.

Joseph Pilates died in 1967, but his wife continued the studio they had opened in New York. Pilates had also trained a lot of students, and some of them went on to open their own studios all around the country.

Eventually Pilates made its way out of the dance world and into the gym. Now millions of people practice Pilates either on its own or in addition to other exercises.

PILATES MOVES

Although Pilates teachers don't refer to asanas, Pilates has specific poses just like yoga. Many look a little different from yoga asanas, though some overlap.

One move is called a teaser. Lie on your back with your knees bent and your feet flat on the floor. Hold your arms behind you on the floor. On an inhalation, bring your arms forward. Then follow with your head and core so that you're halfway to your knees. This move works the **abdominal** muscles, so you should feel the stretch near your stomach. Then slowly lower yourself down without letting gravity do all the work.

Another move is called the corkscrew, which works the abdominals and legs. Lie on your back with your arms out at the side. Straighten your legs and point them toward the ceiling while keeping them together. Draw a circle with them (together) and keep your hips on the floor. Do that several times, then switch directions of the circle. Bring your legs gently back to the ground.

The crisscross also works the abdominals and legs. Start out lying

You should be able to find yoga and Pilates classes in pretty much every community.

Yoga & Pilates

Make Connections: Becoming a Yoga Teacher

 After years of practice, you might decide you want to become a yoga instructor! There isn't one way to become a teacher, and there isn't only one organization that certifies all yoga teachers to practice. Some people work with one teacher to learn how to teach themselves, and to get even better at yoga. Other people attend classes that meet every week for several months in order to get certified by an organization. Still other people go to intensive training schools where they get certified after just a few weeks. Most organizations that offer certification require a certain number of hours of training before someone can start teaching.

on your back with your hands behind your head forming a pillow. Lift your head and shoulders off the ground and bring your knees a little way toward your chest without letting them lie on your chest. Straighten out your right leg while keeping your left leg bent. Twist and bring your right elbow to touch the left knee and hold for a couple seconds. Repeat on the other side with your left leg straight and your left elbow touching the right knee. Continue going back and forth while exhaling as you hold your elbow and knee together.

These are just a small sampling of the many Pilates moves you'll find in a class. They're challenging, but also fun and exhilarating!

WHERE TO FIND YOGA AND PILATES

For thousands of years, yoga teachers—or yogis—have passed down their knowledge to yoga students. Today, you can find many yoga teachers willing to teach new and continuing students all over the world.

Text-Dependent Questions

1. How are yoga and Pilates similar? How are they different?
2. What is meditation and how does it apply to yoga?
3. How long ago was yoga created? What about Pilates?
4. Name two kinds of yoga and describe them.
5. Where might you find a Pilates class in your community?

Many cities and even smaller towns have yoga studios that offer several different classes. One teacher may have her own studio, or several yoga teachers may teach together at one studio, each with his own style of yoga and way of running class.

Studios usually offer beginner classes for people who have never done yoga before, or who are just starting out and have only gone to a few classes. They also offer intermediate classes for students who want to move on, as well as more advanced classes for students who have been practicing for years.

You may also be able to find a Pilates studio, but it's worth it to check out yoga studios to see if they offer a Pilates class or two, since they're similar and often attract the same students.

Gyms like the YMCA usually have some fitness classes in addition to their equipment rooms. Yoga and Pilates are regularly featured as classes through gyms. Community education centers might also have yoga and Pilates classes.

Some schools are even offering yoga and Pilates classes. Gym classes are moving beyond the traditional games and sports, and are trying out activities such as these. Colleges and universities also have yoga and Pilates classes and even courses.

Research Project

Choose one style of yoga and write a short research report on it. You may choose one of the styles listed in this chapter, or find another that you're interested in in learning more about. Write a paragraph about what makes the type unique, along with a paragraph or two about its history, and any other information you think is important to understand what it's all about.

Finally, you can even find yoga and Pilates online. Many websites offer videos for free or for a small payment. You can practice yoga and Pilates right in your own room, and you can choose from a huge range of classes and teachers to find the ones that are right for you.

Words to Understand

 **consistently:** Done in the same way over and over.
repetitive: Done again and again, usually too many times.
diabetes: A disease where your body is unable to use sugar normally to produce energy.
stroke: A burst or blocked blood vessel in your brain.
potential: Able to be something in the future.
restricting: Limiting.

Chapter Two

How Do Yoga and Pilates Contribute to Fitness?

Both yoga and Pilates have many health benefits. They work over time to make practitioners stronger, more flexible, and feeling great.

CORE STRENGTH

Core muscles make up a big part of your body. Core muscles are located in the trunk of the body—anything that isn't the head, neck, arms, or legs. Core muscles include the abdominals, which are stomach muscles

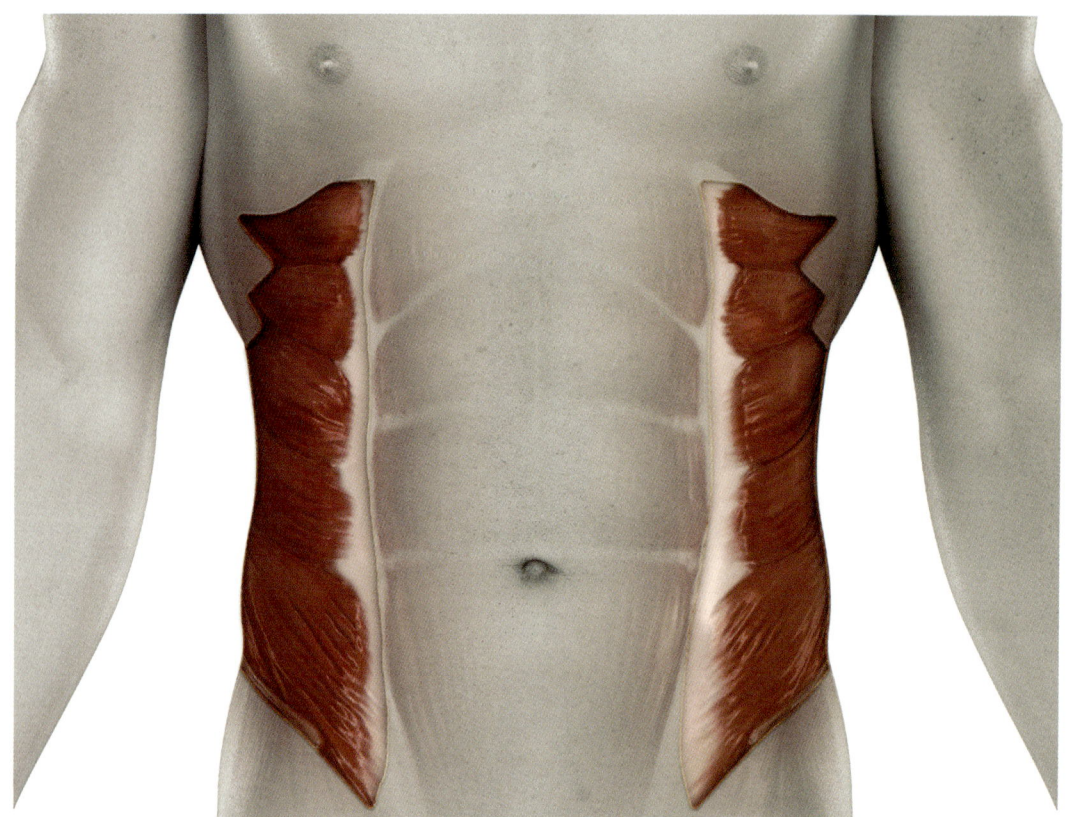

These are the oblique muscles, which you use whenever you twist or bend.

that connect the upper and lower parts of the core. The obliques are another major muscle group in the core, located at the waist, which aid in twisting and bending. Tiny muscles along the spine called erector spinae help you stand up, twist, and bend as well.

The core contains and protects internal organs like the lungs, heart, and stomach. The muscles work together with bones—the ribs and spine—to keep you upright and to protect these organs from harm. Core muscles also give you stability and help you move around during ordinary activities. Weak core muscles make it harder to do everyday movements, such as standing up, bending over, or twisting to reach something above your head.

Yoga & Pilates

Both Pilates and yoga strengthen core muscles, although Pilates focuses on core strength almost exclusively. The moves you perform in Pilates rely heavily on the muscles in your core to hold yourself up. Most Pilates poses are done while lying down so that the core muscles have to resist gravity.

When you first start Pilates or yoga, you may find all the core-muscle work really challenging. But over time, and with practice, you'll find the moves easier and easier because you're building up strength in those muscles.

Other things may be easier as well. Everyday activities will be no trouble at all, and you may also get better at sports. Many sports involve core muscle movement, such as gymnastics, tennis and other racket sports, and volleyball. A stronger core means a stronger performance in these sorts of sports.

A stronger core can also lead to better posture. Posture is the position you're in when you're standing or sitting up. Many people have poor posture, and slouch over when standing or sitting. A weak core makes slouching a lot easier than standing or sitting up straight, but it's not as healthy for your skeleton or muscles. With core exercises, you'll be able to stand and sit up straight without much effort.

LIMB STRENGTH

The core muscles aren't the only muscles in the body. The health and strength of arm and leg muscles are important too. Pilates works on these muscles a little, but yoga is the better exercise system for strengthening arms and legs.

Yoga has a lot of standing poses that focus on leg strength. You'll be bending your legs in ways that make supporting the body more challenging. Arm and leg balances also work on limb strength. Keep in mind that yoga and Pilates work on strength more gently and slowly than other activities like weight lifting. However, one scientific study has shown that young adults who practiced yoga twice a week for eight weeks increased their arm strength by 19 to 31 percent, and leg strength by 28 percent.

Yoga poses like these build flexibility. You probably won't be able to do them right away, but yoga classes are designed to help you build flexibility gradually, so that you can do harder and harder poses.

Yoga & Pilates

Strong arms and legs are beneficial in ways similar to a strong core. If you play sports that involve arm and leg strength (and not many sports don't!), you may see an improvement in your performance. A stronger throwing arm will help you out in baseball or softball, while stronger legs will help you go faster while swimming.

Everyday activities might also get easier. That thirty-pound box of books you have to carry will be no sweat with stronger arms. And that run you promised to do with your friend will be less daunting with stronger legs.

FLEXIBILITY

Flexibility is the range of motion someone has in her muscles, connective tissues, and joints. A person who is very flexible will have a wide range of motion, and will be able to do things like touch his toes, do back bends, and link his arms behind his back.

Some people are naturally more flexible than others. However, most people today don't move around enough or get enough exercise, which makes them lose flexibility. Most of us spend a lot of time sitting, whether at a desk or on a sofa. Luckily, people can improve flexibility by practicing.

Yoga and Pilates are both great ways to increase flexibility. You're probably not used to moving your body in the ways that yoga and Pilates require. Yoga especially can involve a lot of bending and twisting that is safe but challenging. The effect of so much new movement is to train your muscles to stretch longer. Over time, you'll notice that many joints and muscles are now able to stretch farther **consistently**, meaning you're more flexible.

Flexibility is similar to strength in that it can prevent injuries. Many injuries are caused by tight muscles that aren't used to moving in extreme ways, especially injuries that happen in sports or while doing other vigorous activity. Having looser, stretchier muscles keeps that from happening as often.

Again, everyday activities will be easier with more flexibility. Sitting in front of the TV or at a desk all the time makes muscles shorter.

You might not notice this until you have to do something else. Then the new movement will reveal just how tight your muscles are! Whether it's climbing a tree or ladder, picking something off the floor, or throwing a Frisbee, a lack of flexibility makes life a little harder. But with flexibility training, all these things and more will become simple and safe.

INJURY PREVENTION AND RECOVERY

There's some evidence that practicing exercises like Pilates and yoga can help people both prevent injuries and heal faster after getting injured. A lot of that has to do with strength and flexibility. If you're more flexible and stronger, you're less likely to get hurt.

A strong core is a great way to prevent injuries, since it provides balance and stability. You may be less likely to fall and hurt yourself with a strong core. Many people end up injuring their backs at some point in their lives, or suffering from chronic back pain. Core exercises like Pilates work on back strength—which is part of core strength—and can lead to a reduced chance of back injury.

You may also prevent **repetitive** injuries. Someone who has to bend and twist all day for a sport, work, or school activity could end up hurting himself by repeating the same motion over and over again. But with a strong core, the repetitive motions cause less stress.

You might think that people who are injured would be better off resting in bed than doing something demanding like yoga or Pilates. But that's only true up to a point. People who are able to move around at least a little may recover faster if they practice gentle exercise, as long as it's the right kind of exercise. Some studies show that people with lower back pain, for example, can recover from their pain by doing gentle yoga or Pilates. Practicing yoga helps them reduce pain and move around more easily.

WEIGHT LOSS

Obesity and overweight are tied to health risks such as **diabetes**, **stroke**, heart disease, and joint pain. The decision to lose weight should

Yoga is a great form of exercise because it can be done by anyone anywhere.

primarily be a health decision, not an attempt to be more beautiful or a better person.

Yoga and Pilates can aid in weight loss, though other exercises lead to faster and larger weight loss. The key to weight loss is to burn more calories through activity than you are consuming. Calories measure how much energy is in food, so a food with a thousand calories has much more energy than a food with one hundred calories. Calories aren't bad—in fact you need around 2,000 calories a day to live. But too many calories lead to weight gain and **potential** health problems.

So, to burn more calories than you consume, you need to either eat fewer calories or burn more. Usually the best method is to do a little of both, depending on your goals. Just **restricting** calories is not generally healthy, and severely restricting them can lead to all sorts of other health problems.

How Do Yoga and Pilates Contribute to Fitness?

Research Project

This chapter mentions that some scientific studies have been conducted to test the health claims of yoga and Pilates. See if you can find one of these studies. You may find the study itself, or a news article that reports the study's findings. Write a short report about what you read. What was the question the study was trying to answer? What was the study's hypothesis (the proposed answer to the question)? How did the scientists conduct the study? What were the results, and what do those results mean? What don't they mean?

Yoga and Pilates help burn some calories. They are great workouts, especially if you don't already have a high level of fitness. They'll help you burn calories slowly and steadily, if you practice yoga and Pilates regularly.

If your goal is major weight loss (and you've talked to a doctor), yoga and Pilates are also great in combination with another sort of activity that burns more calories. Running, swimming, and playing sports like soccer or field hockey will help you lose more weight faster. For

Make Connections: Some More Benefits

People claim that yoga and Pilates have even more health benefits. Scientific studies haven't proven these claims yet, but individuals' stories may tell you otherwise. Practitioners have used yoga to find relief from asthma, high blood pressure, arthritis, poor function of the immune system, multiple sclerosis, and neck pain.

34   Yoga & Pilates

1. What is the core, and what muscles make up the core?
2. Why is core strength important?
3. How will limb strength improve sports performance?
4. Can yoga and Pilates help prevent injuries, and if so, how?
5. How can yoga and Pilates help with healthy weight-loss goals?

variety and to work on different sorts of strength along with flexibility, yoga and Pilates are good additions to these sorts of exercises.

FITNESS FOR ANYONE

One of the great things about yoga and Pilates is that just about anyone can do them. Even people who are very young, elderly, injured, or out of shape can start a yoga or Pilates practice, and quickly see results. Many studios and gyms offer yoga classes that are less strenuous than others. There are classes designed for people who can't stand, who are pregnant, or who are recovering from an injury. There are also classes for children, athletes, and more.

Yoga teachers often stress that students should do what they are able to in class, without worrying if it is "correct" or not. The teacher offers guidelines, but people's postures will look a little different depending on their bodies. Yoga classes are usually very accepting environments, and students are free to skip on asanas they can't do because of physical limitations. So no matter who you are and what you can do, yoga and even Pilates will push you safely and in a healthy way toward fitness.

Words to Understand

hydrated: Having enough water in your body for it to work properly.
chronic: Ongoing or lasting a long time.
osteoporosis: A disease where your bones become brittle and weak.
productive: Achieving a good or strong result.
motivated: Having the drive to start or continue doing something.

Chapter Three
GEAR AND SAFETY FOR YOGA AND PILATES

One of the reasons yoga and Pilates are so popular is because they don't require a lot of equipment. You don't need to buy a lot of fancy things in order to practice, and you don't even have to spend a lot of money taking classes.

Another reason people like these exercise systems so much is because they are generally safe. Neither yoga nor Pilates causes a lot of injuries, particularly since they are both low-impact exercises. High-impact activities like running put a lot of pressure on joints and bones, which can cause injuries easily. Yoga and Pilates are much gentler,

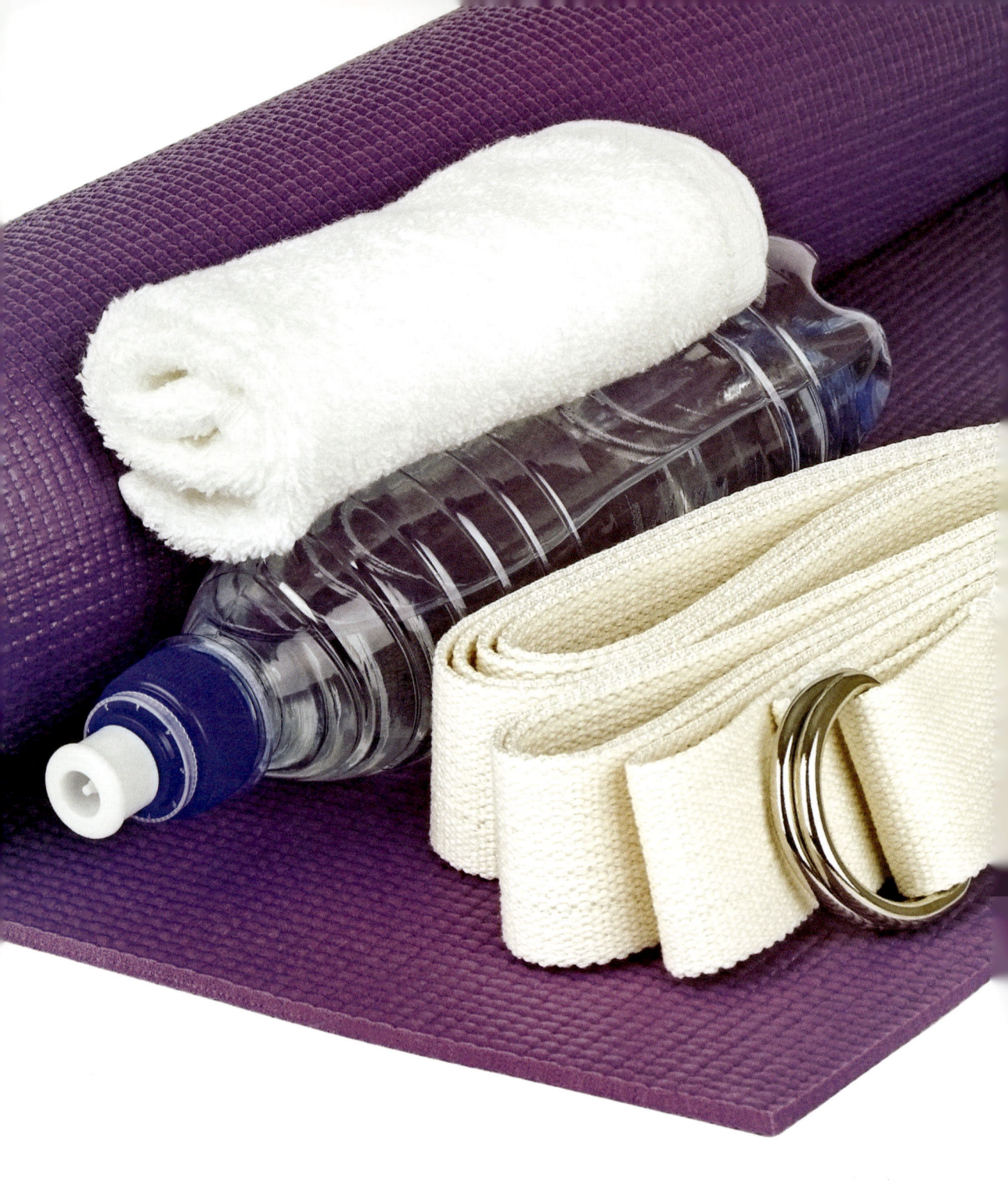

Yoga doesn't require a lot of equipment. A mat, a strap, a towel, and a water bottle, and you're good to go!

Yoga & Pilates

even while they are providing a good workout and contributing toward fitness.

LIMITED EQUIPMENT

To start practicing yoga or Pilates, all you really need is a floor mat. Technically, you could practice them without a mat, but it would be a lot more painful, and you might slip around a lot. Floor mats keep you from sliding around on a slippery floor, and they keep your knees, butt, hands, elbows, and feet cushioned while exercising.

Mats cost as little as $10 for a basic one that works just as well as a more expensive mat. Once you've got that, you're ready to go! You may not even have to buy one if your gym, studio, or school offers them for free.

You can choose to buy a few more items if you want. Some yoga poses will require a blanket with which to support yourself. Poses that involve your knees will be safer and less painful with a blanket under them, as will back bends. Similarly, foam blocks will help make some poses more comfortable and safer. If you're bending in an awkward position and can't quite reach the floor for support, you may be able to set down a block to use it as support instead.

The only other equipment you may need in yoga is a strap. A few teachers will have you use a strap to make stretches more intense and to hold poses more easily. Straps are made of cotton and have a simple buckle to hold them in place. Many studios offer students the use of straps for free, and may also offer blocks and blankets.

Some stores try to sell fancy Pilates equipment that you don't really need. Some teachers use exercise balls, bands, or rings, but they aren't usually necessary. The beauty of Pilates and yoga is that you're using the weight of your body to exercise, rather than a lot of equipment.

You also may want to have a water bottle and a towel handy. If you sweat a lot, you can wipe off with a towel. And staying **hydrated** while exercising is always a great idea.

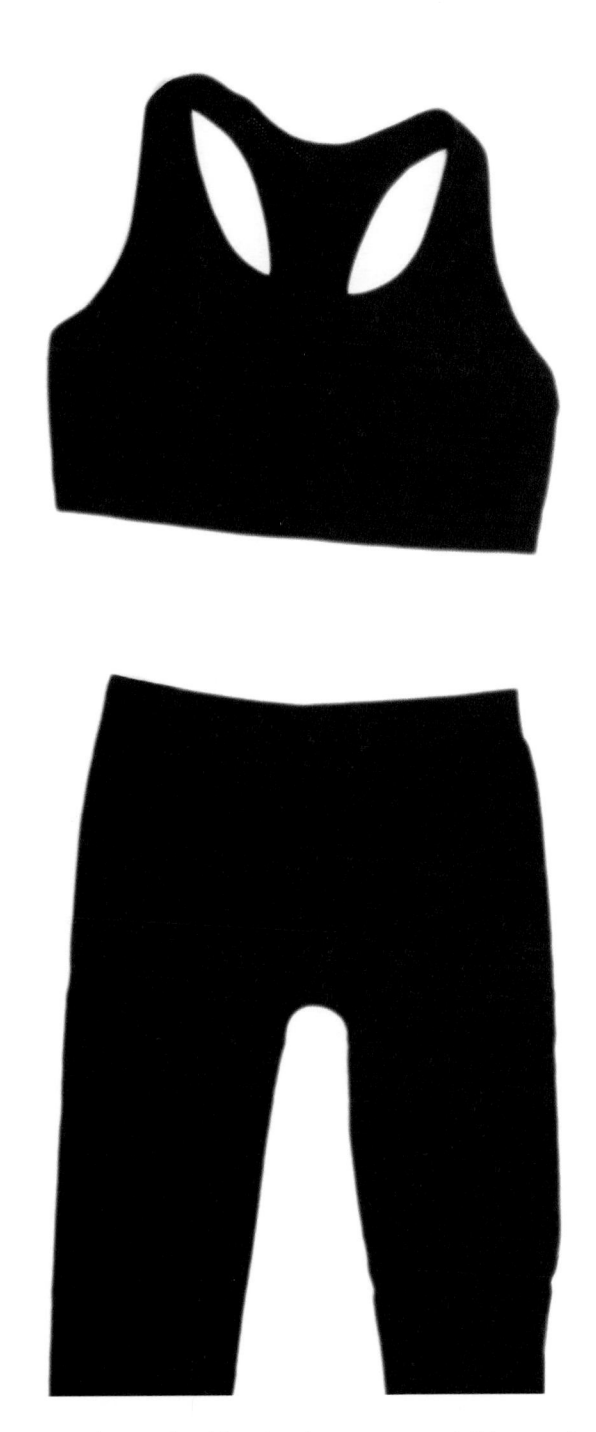

Lots of people wear stretchy outfits like this for yoga and Pilates class—but it doesn't really matter what you wear, so long as it lets you move comfortably.

Yoga & Pilates

CLOTHES

You're not going to want to wear your usual street clothes while practicing yoga or Pilates. Keep your clothing comfortable and easy to move around in. People often wear athletic shorts or leggings on the bottom (so no jeans!) and tighter t-shirts or tank tops on top. Keep in mind that you may be upside down for some poses, so you don't want your shirt falling over your head!

Don't worry about shoes—yoga and Pilates practitioners take off their shoes and socks. You don't need any fancy sneakers for these exercises.

If the place where you're exercising is cold, layer up. Wear comfy long-sleeved shirts or sweaters when you first start. As you warm up, you can take off some layers, and as you cool down again toward the end of the practice, you can put them back on.

CLASSES

The only other thing you may have to invest in is a class. If you want to practice yoga or Pilates regularly with a bunch of other people around, you'll need to find a class you can take. Classes run from about $5 to $20 per session, depending on the class and where you live. If you hunt around, you may also be able to find a free class or two. Many studios offer a deal when you first sign up with them. You might get unlimited classes for two weeks for $25 or two free classes to use whenever you want.

Starting with a real-life instructor is helpful for beginners. That way, you start off knowing the proper way to approach certain poses, and you'll get to see just what yoga or Pilates is all about. You can get feedback from the teacher, and let him or her know about any physical restrictions you have.

However, if classes don't sound right for you or are too expensive, you can also do them at home. You can find lots of yoga and Pilates DVDs for sale, or you can buy them to download online. As long as

Some yoga poses are more advanced than others. A pose like this requires not only flexibility but also a lot of muscle strength. Don't try to do anything you're not ready for!

Yoga & Pilates

you have enough space and a mat to practice on, you can exercise at home.

For an even cheaper experience, you can find plenty of free yoga and Pilates classes online. Search for "free yoga/Pilates classes" and see what comes up. There are actually whole websites devoted to free classes, and certified and talented teachers usually lead them.

BASIC SAFETY

Yoga and Pilates are generally very safe ways to exercise. But as with anything, you could get hurt if you push your body too hard. Yoga classes especially give you room to back off from a pose if you feel like you'll get hurt. You just need to know when to back off and when to keep going, as with any exercise.

Yoga and Pilates definitely push students to their maximum at times. Teachers should provide some guidance about when poses are too hard and you need to ease up, as well as when you should keep going. In general, you may feel some intense sensations like your muscles seeming warm or even shaking, but you shouldn't feel pain. Any sort of sharp pain, especially in your lower back or neck, is an indication that you should get out of whatever pose you're in.

Most yoga and Pilates classes build in some time to warm up and slow down. You don't start in on the hard stuff right away. You get some time to stretch first, and then work up to more intense poses. At the end, you'll do more gentle poses and will end with meditation or just lying on the ground. Teachers may also build in counter poses that are helpful to balance out challenging poses. After doing some back-bending poses, for example, your teacher may have you lie on your back with your knees on your chest, to work out your spine.

You should also be aware of how far you're stretching your muscles, especially if you're just starting out. At first, your muscles might be tight. You'll become more flexible over time, but you'll have to stretch them out a little bit at a time. If you stretch them too fast, you could pull a muscle or connective tissue, which is painful and will prevent you from doing yoga or Pilates for a little while.

An older person or anyone with a health condition should talk to a doctor before beginning any exercise program—but in most cases, yoga can be adapted so that is good for pretty much anyone.

Yoga & Pilates

In general, avoid starting with advanced yoga and Pilates classes. You might want to start doing handstands and two-hour Pilates sessions right away, but you could injure yourself and burn out on exercise because of frustration. Start off with a beginner's class, and work your way up. If you're really excited by these systems of exercise, you'll probably improve quickly and start doing more complicated poses soon enough. But if you push yourself too hard at the beginning, you might end up with an injury that keeps you from exercising for several weeks or months.

WHO SHOULDN'T DO YOGA AND PILATES?

There are forms of yoga for just about everyone, but some people should take more care when practicing either yoga or Pilates. People with health problems like heart disease, high blood pressure, eye problems, **chronic** back or other muscle pain, or **osteoporosis** should avoid some of the poses regularly found in yoga and Pilates classes. Yoga and Pilates could make these problems worse.

Women who are pregnant should also think about how much yoga and Pilates they feel comfortable doing, and how much is safe. There are special yoga classes for pregnant women, which involve poses that are safe and beneficial. More intense poses may not be a good idea, particularly for women who are later on in their pregnancies.

Anyone recovering from an injury and the elderly should also be careful about doing too much yoga or Pilates, although some might be helpful. Again, you may be able to find special classes for people with certain kinds of injuries, health problems, or for the elderly. There's even chair yoga!

It's a good idea to talk with your doctor before you start any fitness program. If you're completely healthy already, there's probably no danger with starting a yoga or Pilates practice—but it's better to be safe than sorry.

If you have any health conditions that might affect your ability to exercise, you should definitely consult a doctor. She will be able to tell

Good nutrition, with foods from each of these groups, is important for building strong bodies.

46 Yoga & Pilates

Make Connections: Exercising Too Much

There is definitely such a thing as exercising too much. Besides risk of injury, exercise can lead to too much weight loss and an unhealthy relationship with the body. A small set of people suffer from a disease called exercise bulimia, in which they exercise in order to burn lots and lots of calories because they think they're fat. They don't eat enough food to keep themselves going, and they can do real damage to their bodies. People with exercise bulimia suffer from a disease and need help to get healthy.

you more about whether doing this sort of exercise will help you or hurt you. For example, if you just threw out your back, your doctor would probably recommend staying away from yoga and Pilates for a while, but he would let you know when it's safe to start again, and when exercise might become beneficial for healing.

DON'T FORGET TO EAT!

Exercise and fitness is only one side of health. You could exercise every day and still be unhealthy if your diet is made up of junk food. Your body needs healthy foods too, not just movement.

Eating healthy food also contributes to making exercise more **productive**. Imagine you've just eaten a huge meal of fried foods and soda, and then try to do Pilates. You're not going to want to exercise, and it's going to be a lot harder. You'd probably rather sit on the couch or take a nap. More healthy eating, however, will give you more energy, not less, and will make you ready to go. You'll be more **motivated** to exercise and move around.

Gear and Safety for Yoga and Pilates 47

Text-Dependent Questions

1. What is the only necessary piece of equipment for yoga and Pilates? What are some optional types of equipment?
2. What are some ways you can find a yoga or Pilates class?
3. Why shouldn't you push yourself too hard when you first start an exercise program?
4. How should someone with an injury approach yoga or Pilates?
5. Identify two basic healthy eating guidelines.

Healthy eating is a pretty easy concept to grasp, even if actually eating healthy isn't always so easy. Some of the basic guidelines for healthy eating are to eat as many fruits and vegetables as possible, add in whole-grain foods instead of refined grains, and make junk food an occasional treat. Healthy eating also involves keeping portions small rather than overeating.

Eat more fruits and vegetables. Try raw fruit for breakfast or snacks, salads for lunch or along with dinner, and cut up carrots and broccoli with dip. Start out with the fruits and vegetables you like—and then try new ones! Scientists say people sometimes need to try a new food nine times before they like it. Vegetable and fruit juices are good (as long as they are 100 percent juice and not mostly water with sugar and flavors added in), but don't rely on juice for your only fruits and vegetables.

Eat grains, which include foods like rice, oats, wheat, and barley. Grains are seeds from certain kinds of plants, which are packed with vitamins and minerals. Whole grains include the whole seed. Refined grains have some of the parts taken out, which removes some of the vitamins and minerals. Whole grains and whole-grain foods are healthier than refined grains and foods made from those. Whole-grain foods

Research Project

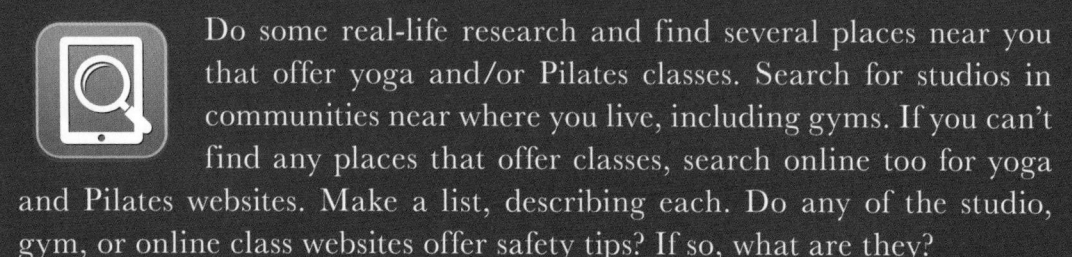

Do some real-life research and find several places near you that offer yoga and/or Pilates classes. Search for studios in communities near where you live, including gyms. If you can't find any places that offer classes, search online too for yoga and Pilates websites. Make a list, describing each. Do any of the studio, gym, or online class websites offer safety tips? If so, what are they?

include oatmeal, whole-wheat bread, brown rice, and whole-wheat pasta. Eat more of these and less refined grain foods, like white bread, white rice, and regular crackers.

In addition to adding in lots of healthy foods to your diet, it's a good idea to take some junk food out. People often think junk food is delicious—that's part of the reason we eat it all the time! But too much junk food can make you feel bloated and tired, and it can lead to long-term health problems like obesity and diabetes. You don't have to cut junk food out of your diet entirely, but try and limit it.

Finally, eating proper portions is part of a healthy diet. Portions are the amount of food you put on your plate and eat in one sitting. Portions shouldn't be heaping, unless you are really hungry. Eat until you're almost full, rather than stuffed and feeling really tired.

All these good-nutrition habits will help you do better when you exercise. Then you'll be able to get all the benefits yoga and Pilates have to offer!

Words to Understand

perseverance: Continuing to try hard, even if you fail at first.
therapy: Treatment for a medical condition.

Chapter Four

What Other Benefits Do Yoga and Pilates Have?

While yoga and Pilates are great for physical fitness, they have a lot more benefits than just that. These exercise systems are also a good way to train your mind, and they have all sorts of good emotional effects. If you're looking for a way to de-stress, calm down, or deal with depression or anxiety, you might turn to yoga or Pilates.

Building a strong body through yoga or Pilates tends to also improve your overall mood and self-concept. These exercise forms make you feel good about yourself!

Yoga & Pilates

MOOD

After just one yoga or Pilates class, you may notice that you're in a better mood than when you started. Any sort of physical activity increases levels of chemicals in your brain that make you feel happier, and yoga and Pilates are no different. Exercise also increases the oxygen levels in the blood through an increased heart rate and deeper breathing, which eventually reach the brain. More oxygen means clearer thinking and an improved mood.

Pay attention to the mood you're in before you start a class, and then see how you feel afterward. If you were feeling sad, anxious, angry, or stressed out, you might notice that you're much calmer. Exercise isn't like magic—you'll still feel difficult emotions sometimes even if you exercise regularly. But exercise can make it easier to deal with those emotions when you do experience them.

SELF-CONFIDENCE

Self-confidence is trust in your ability to do things and to be a good person. You can feel self-confident about your intelligence, your values, your appearance, and many other things.

Many people lack self-confidence, but fortunately it's something we can learn. Exercise is one way to improve self-confidence, because hard work pays off with results, whether you're trying to get in shape or trying to lose weight for health reasons.

When you first start out with yoga or Pilates, you might not be able to do a whole lot. One class might be really difficult, and you might feel like you're way behind everyone else. With **perseverance**, you'll start to improve. You may not even notice how much you're improving, but one day you'll think back to when you started your practice. At first, one pose might have been almost impossible, but two months in, you can do it with no problems. You're ready to move on to even more challenging

What Other Benefits Do Yoga and Pilates Have?

Most yoga classes end with a time when you totally relax your body. This deep relaxation is a good way to fight stress.

Yoga & Pilates

poses. You feel a sense of accomplishment and pride, and a boost of self-confidence as well.

STRESS REDUCTION

These days, everyone seems to be busy and stressed out all the time. Making room for exercise in your weekly schedule can combat some of the stress of everyday living. Yoga and Pilates are particularly well-suited for calming down and distressing.

A lot of stress is worrying about the past or the future. We forget about what we're doing right now, and get distracted by the mistakes we made in the past, or all the things we have to do in the future. Yoga and Pilates are all about concentrating on what's happening right now. When you're working out and trying to do challenging poses, you don't have time to think about other things! The meditation techniques introduced in yoga are also great for letting go and being in the moment, so make the most out of those parts of class.

The focus on breathing in yoga and Pilates also helps calm the mind and reduce stress. As you breathe more slowly and more deeply, your mind stops racing, your heartbeat slows down, and you get more oxygen to your body and brain. All those things physically and mentally calm you down, so you can stop stressing out for at least a little while.

Scientists suggest that stress negatively impacts health. People are more likely to catch colds and other ordinary illnesses because their immune systems aren't working as well when they're stressed out. They also may be more likely to suffer from serious health problems. So exercise is good for your body in more ways than one.

FIGHTING DEPRESSION AND ANXIETY

Yoga and Pilates—and exercise in general—can also fight off more serious problems like depression and anxiety.

Being a part of a class can keep you motivated. The more exercise you fit into your life, the healthier and happier you'll be!

Yoga & Pilates

Text-Dependent Questions

1. How does exercise improve your mood?
2. What is self-confidence? What does exercise have to do with self-confidence?
3. Why are yoga and Pilates beneficial in fighting stress?
4. What is depression, and what are some ways of treating it? What is exercise's connection to depression?
5. What is anxiety? How can starting yoga or Pilates calm anxiety?

Depression is an overwhelming sense of sadness and lack of energy. There are different levels of depression, and some need to be treated with ***therapy*** and special medicine called antidepressants. Exercise is also a way to fight depression, because of the chemicals it releases in the brain, called endorphins. Endorphins lessen the feeling of pain. They're also calming and improve mood. The more you exercise, the more endorphins get released.

When someone is depressed, he may find it hard to get motivated and exercise. But since yoga and Pilates can be practiced at home, alone, there's a better chance for some people to take the first step and start exercising.

Anxiety is a related emotional issue and involves feeling nervous or uneasy for extended periods of time. Anxiety is more than just stress, but it can be treated with exercise, just like stress can. And because yoga and Pilates focus on concentration, awareness of the body, and deep breathing, they're particularly good at fighting anxiety. The meditation focus of many forms of yoga is also a great way to reduce anxiety.

What Other Benefits Do Yoga and Pilates Have?

Research Project

There is a whole science behind how exercise affects mental health. Choose mood, stress, depression, or anxiety, and do more investigation into just how exercise influences these states. Find out how exercise affects a particular aspect of emotions, and some of the scientific processes that are changed. You'll want to focus specifically on the brain, and the changes exercise causes in the brain.

In fact, the benefits of yoga and Pilates are almost endless! You can't beat these exercises for improving mood, fighting stress, gaining strength, and becoming more flexible. Plus, yoga and Pilates are fun and challenging, and never boring. Choosing to start practicing yoga or Pilates is a step in the right direction toward mental and physical health, and a way to take control of your fitness.

FIND OUT MORE

In Books

Biegel, Gina. *The Stress Reduction Workbook for Teens.* Oakland, CA: New Harbinger Publications, 2009.

Chryssicas, Mary Kaye. *Breathe: Yoga for Teens.* New York: DK Publishing, 2007.

Johnson, Cliff. *Inner Peace in a Busy World: A Young Person's Guide to Meditation.* Bloomington, IN: Author House, 2007.

Kennedy, Denis, Sian Williams, and Dominique Jansen. *Pilates for Beginners.* New York: Rosen Publishing, 2011.

Purperhart, Helen. *Yoga Exercises for Teens.* Alameda, CA.: Hunter House Books, 2009.

Online

Nutrition and Fitness for Teens
www.pamf.org/teen/health/nutrition

TeensHealth: Pilates
kidshealth.org/teen/food_fitness/exercise/pilates.html

TeensHealth: Yoga
kidshealth.org/teen/food_fitness/exercise/yoga.html

WebMD: The Benefits of Pilates
www.webmd.com/fitness-exercise/features/the-benefits-of-pilates

Yoga Journal
www.yogajournal.com

SERIES GLOSSARY OF KEY TERMS

abs: Short for abdominals. The muscles in the middle of your body, located over your stomach and intestines.

aerobic: A process by which energy is steadily released using oxygen. Aerobic exercise focuses on breathing and exercising for a long time.

anaerobic: When lots of energy is quickly released, without using oxygen. You can't do anaerobic exercises for a very long time.

balance: Your ability to stay steady and upright.

basal metabolic rate: How many calories your body burns naturally just by breathing and carrying out other body processes.

bodybuilding: Exercising specifically to get bigger, stronger muscles.

calories: The units of energy that your body uses. You get calories from food and you use them up when you exercise.

carbohydrates: The foods that your body gets most of its energy from. Common foods high in carbohydrates include sugars and grains.

cardiovascular system: Your heart and blood vessels.

circuit training: Rapidly switching from one exercise to another in a cycle. Circuit training helps build endurance in many different muscle groups.

circulatory system: The system of blood vessels in your body, which brings oxygen and nutrients to your cells and carries waste products away.

cool down: A gentle exercise that helps your body start to relax after a workout.

core: The muscles of your torso, including your abs and back muscles.

cross training: When an athlete trains for a sport she normally doesn't play, to exercise any muscle groups she might be weak in.

dehydration: When you don't have enough water in your body. When you exercise, you lose water by sweating, and it's important to replace it.

deltoids: The thick muscles covering your shoulder joint.
energy: The power your body needs to do things like move around and keep you alive.
endurance: The ability to keep going for a long time.
flexibility: How far you can bend, or how far your muscles can stretch.
glutes: Short for gluteals, the muscles in your buttocks.
hydration: Taking in more water to keep from getting dehydrated.
isometric: An exercise that you do without moving, by holding one position.
isotonic: An exercise you do by moving your muscles.
lactic acid: A chemical that builds up in your muscles after you exercise. It causes a burning feeling during anaerobic exercises.
lats: Short for latissimus dorsi, the large muscles along your back.
metabolism: How fast you digest food and burn energy.
muscle: The parts of your body that contract and expand to allow you to move.
nervous system: Made up of your brain, spinal cord, and nerves, which carry messages between your brain, spinal cord, and the rest of your body.
nutrition: The chemical parts of the food you eat that your body needs to survive and use energy.
obliques: The muscles to either side of your stomach, under your ribcage.
pecs: Short for pectorals, the muscles on your chest.
quads: Short for quadriceps, the large muscle on the front of your upper leg and thigh.
reps: How many times you repeat an anaerobic exercise in a row.
strength: The power of your muscles.
stretching: Pulling on your muscles to make them longer. Stretching before you exercise can keep you flexible and prevent injuries.
warm up: A light exercise you do before a workout to get your body ready for harder exercise.
weight training: Exercises that involve lifting heavy weights to increase your strength and endurance.

INDEX

anxiety 51, 55, 57–58
asanas 11, 15, 19, 21, 35

back bend 19, 31, 39
back pain 32
balance 15, 19, 29, 32, 43
bending 28–29, 31, 39, 43
Buddhism 13
bulimia 47
breathing 11, 15, 17, 53, 55, 57

calories 33–34, 47
classes 18, 22–25, 30, 35, 37, 41, 43, 45, 49, 54
clothes 41
core 11, 21, 27–29, 31–32, 35

depression 51, 55, 57–58
doctor 34, 44–45, 47
DVDs 41

eating 6–7, 47–49
elderly 35, 45
endorphins 57
equipment 15, 24, 37–39, 48
exercise 9–10, 19, 21, 29, 31–33, 35, 37, 39, 41, 43–45, 47–49, 51–53, 55–58

fitness 6–7, 9, 19, 21, 24, 27, 34–35, 39, 45, 47, 51, 58
flexibility 9, 19, 30–32, 35, 42
floor mat 39

gym 9, 21, 24, 35, 39, 49

healing 47
Hinduism 13

Indus Valley 13
injuries 31–32, 35, 37, 45, 47–48

junk food 47–49

limbs 29, 35

meditation 11, 15–16, 24, 43, 55, 57
mood 52–53, 57–58
muscles 11, 18, 20–21, 27–29, 31–32, 35, 42–43, 45

Patanjali 13, 15
Pilates, Joseph 9, 11, 18–19, 21–25, 27, 29, 31–35, 37, 39–41, 43, 45, 47–49, 51–53, 55, 57–58

portion 48–49
poses 11, 15, 17–21, 29–30, 39, 41–43, 45, 53, 55
posture 11, 17, 29, 35

religion 13

safety 37, 43, 49
self-confidence 53, 55, 57
sports 9, 24, 29, 31–32, 34–35
strength 9, 19, 27, 29, 31–32, 35, 42, 58
stress 11, 32, 35, 51, 54–55, 57–58

studio 21, 24, 35, 39, 41, 49

teacher 13, 21, 23–25, 35, 39, 41, 43
twisting 28, 31

water 36, 38–39, 48
website 25, 43, 49
weight loss 32–34, 47
weight 9, 19, 29, 32–35, 39, 47, 53
whole grain 48

ABOUT THE AUTHOR AND THE CONSULTANT

Sara James is a writer and blogger. She writes educational books for children on a variety of topics, including health, history, and current events.

Diane H. Hart, Nationally Certified Fitness Professional and Health Specialist, has designed and implemented fitness and wellness programs for more than twenty years. She is a master member of the International Association of Fitness Professionals, and a health specialist for Blue Shield of Northeastern New York, HealthNow, and Palladian Health. In 2010, Diane was elected president of the National Association for Health and Fitness (NAHF), a nonprofit organization that exists to improve the quality of life for individuals in the United States through the promotion of physical fitness, sports, and healthy lifestyles. NAHF accomplishes this work by fostering and supporting state governors and state councils and coalitions that promote and encourage regular physical activity. NAHF is also the national sponsor of Employee Health and Fitness Month, the largest global workplace health and fitness event each May. American College of Sports Medicine (ACSM) has been a strategic partner with NAHF since 2009.

PICTURE CREDITS

Fotolia.com:
- 8: Rob
- 10: rudall30
- 16: olly
- 17: George Dolgikh
- 18: Shay Yizhak
- 20: Michael Gray
- 22: Visionsi
- 26: auremar
- 28: CLIPAREA.com
- 30: furmananna
- 33: yanlev
- 36: Scott Griessel
- 38: Ekaterina Garyuk
- 40: Africa Studio
- 42: Elena Ray
- 44: magann
- 46: onoontour
- 50: luminastock
- 52: Paul Hakimata
- 54: contrastwerkstatt
- 56: WavebreakmediaMicro

14: Library of Congress

North Providence Union Free Library
1810 Mineral Spring Avenue
North Providence, RI 02904
353-5600